D1262064

Executive Producers: John Christianson and Ron Berry
Art Design: Gary Currant
Layout: Currant Design Group and Best Impression Graphics

HOW i FEEL

SAD

by Marcia Leonard
illustrated by Bartholomew

This little girl can't find her doll.
She feels sad.

This little boy feels sad, too.
His parents are going out,
and he has to stay home
with the babysitter.

This little girl is sad because
she dropped her ice cream.

Would that make you sad?
Can you make a sad face?

There are different reasons for being sad,
and there are different kinds of sadness.

Can you think of something
that makes you sad?

You might feel a *little* bit sad
when a play date is over
and your friend has to go home.

Are you sad when a play date is over?

But you'd probably feel *very* sad
if your grandparents moved far away.

How would you feel
if that happened to you?

It's okay to feel sad,
and it's okay to cry.
But after a while,
you'll be ready to feel better.

You can comfort yourself
by hugging a stuffed animal
or a cuddle blanket.

Or you can read a favorite book
or play a favorite game.

But best of all,
you can talk to Mommy or Daddy
about what's making you sad,
and they can help you make
the sad feelings go away.